JUNE SOBEL

B Is for Bulldozer

A CONSTRUCTION ABC

ILLUSTRATED BY
MELISSA IWAI

VOYAGER BOOKS
HARCOURT, INC.
Orlando Austin New York San Diego London

For information about permission to reproduce selections from this book,
please write to Permissions, Houghton Mifflin Harcourt Publishing
Company 215 Park Avenue South NY NY 10003

www.hmhbooks.com

First Voyager Books edition 2006

Voyager Books is a trademark of Harcourt, Inc., registered in the
United States of America and/or other jurisdictions.

The Library of Congress has cataloged the hardcover edition as follows:
Sobel, June.
B is for bulldozer: a construction ABC/by June Sobel;
illustrated by Melissa Iwai.
p. cm.
Summary: As children watch over the course of a year,
builders construct a roller coaster using tools and materials
that begin with each letter of the alphabet.
[1. Roller coasters—Fiction. 2. Building—Fiction. 3. Construction
equipment—Fiction. 4. Alphabet. 5. Stories in rhyme.]
I. Iwai, Melissa, ill. II. Title.
PZ7.S685228Bi 2003
[E]—dc21   2001006869
ISBN 978-0-15-202250-1
ISBN 978-0-15-205774-9 pb

SCP 10 9 8
4500391722

The illustrations in this book were done in acrylic on board.
The text type was set in Bernhard Gothic Medium.
The display type was set in Bernhard Antique and Stencil.
Color separations by Colourscan Co. Pte. Ltd., Singapore
Printed in China by RR Donnelley
Production supervision by Ginger Boyer
Designed by Linda Lockowitz

To Adam Raudonis—
my inspiration

—J. S.

For my dad,
the best builder I know

—M. I.

COMING SOON!

WONDERLAND

Do you see the Asphalt for paving the road,

or the big shiny
Bulldozer
pushing a load?

I see a Crane
way up high
in the sky,

and a rusty red
Dump truck
rumbling by.

Here comes an **E**xcavator to dig a huge hole.

Nearby there's a **F**orklift hauling a pole.

Let's look for
the Grader
on the roadbed,

and a man with a
Hard hat protecting
his head.

I spy an I beam made out of steel,

and a **J**ackhammer making
a noise you can feel.

Hear that **K**a-boom?
What a loud sound!

KEEP OU

Look! That huge Loader
scoops dirt from the ground.

Watch people swing
Mallets at a swift pace,

pounding in Nails
to hold parts in their place.

Let's find the **O**perator at the controls,

guiding the Pipes
into the holes.

The welders won't Quit
till the metal is bent,

and the new
safety Rails are
placed in cement.

See the Scaffolds come down before our eyes,

while workers pack up
their Tools and supplies.

The **U**nderpass barrier
is taken away.

WONDERLAND

★ ★ ★

GRAND OPENING

Now **V**isitors enter—
it's opening day!

The construction **W**ork
is finally done.

Our eXcitement grows—
we're ready for fun!

For more than a **Y**ear we've watched the park bloom.

Now hold on tight....
Here we go....
Get set to...

Z-O-O-M!!!!!!!!